mari loves reading

To: Dylan

Happy Reading

♡

Marva

Written by Marva Carty

Illustrated by TullipStudio

Mari Loves Reading

Disclaimer

This is a work of fiction. Names, characters, businesses, places, events, and incidents are either the products
of the author's imagination or used in a fictitious manner.
Any resemblance to actual persons, living or dead,
or actual events is purely coincidental.

License Notes

(Paperback) ISBN 978-1-7398328-4-1

Illustrated by TullipStudio

Publisher's Name: MangoLime Publishing

Publisher's address: 27 Old Gloucester Street, London,

WC1N 3AX

Acknowledgements

**To those that came before and told
their stories, thank you.
To those with stories yet to be told,
we encourage you.**

Meet Mari. She is seven and lives on a beautiful island. She loves school, playtime with her friends, and mangoes!

There is one thing Mari loves
to do more than anything.

Mari loves reading!

She loves small books and BIG BOOKS.

Anywhere and anytime.

She loves books that are full
of interesting facts. Did you know dogs can
smell 100,000 times better than humans?
Or that most people cannot lick their
elbows? Try it!

Her favourite place to read
is in the school library.

Miss told the class that they were going
to start a reading challenge today.
She said that whoever read
the most books from the library that
month would win an amazing prize.

Mari was sure she would win. No one could read more books than her!

Her favourite stories were about clever detectives and action heroes who rescued everyone and saved the day.

She said to Kevin, "This is great!.
I can't wait to start the challenge!"

But Kevin replied, "I never find books I like.
I just want to play with my LEGO
or on my tablet."

Mari shook her head and asked,
"So, what do you want to read about,
Kevin?" Kevin replied, "Lots of things!
I want to learn how to design computers
or make a famous invention from
somebody who looks like me."

Mari asks Mummy to help them find some books that Miss could buy for the library.

Miss shook her head, "Mari, the school has no more money to buy books right now."

What were Mari and Kevin going to do? Then Mari had an idea. "Let's have a cake sale. Daddy and Mummy can help us bake. We can tell everyone to bring extra money to buy our treats at break time so we can get more books!", she said.

Everyone brought money to school to buy the yummy snacks. They had sugar cakes, coconut tart, mango bread, sweetbread, mango chow, cupcakes, fudge, and fruit juices.

They took the money to Mari's favourite
bookstore. Mister Best, the bookstore
owner, helped Kevin choose some fun books
that he would enjoy reading.

Kevin raced home to start reading.
Sometimes, he read with Mari or his dad.
On other days, he read alone.
Sometimes, he read so much that
he even forgot when it was dinner time!

Mari read about clever detectives,
powerful mermaids under the sea,
famous people in history,
and travelling to different countries.

Kevin found heroes old and new in his books. He got great ideas for new inventions and learned new ways to play his favourite sports. He couldn't wait to try out everything he had read about.

When the challenge was over, it was no surprise when Miss announced that the winner was Mari!

Kevin won a special prize for his hard work in reading and helping the library. They split the box and shared some of the prizes with the class.

The End

Making Sugar Cakes

Ingredients:

 4 cups sugar

 1 cup water

4 cups fine shredded unsweetened coconut

 1/2 teaspoon cream of tartar

 1 teaspoon almond extract

 food coloring (optional)

 syrup

Quantities:

 bowl

 stirrer

 spoon

 pan

 knife

 tray

WARNING!
You need a grown-up to help

1 Boil sugar and water to form a light syrup.

2 When bubbles the size of small pearls appear, add grated coconut and cream of tartar.

3 When the coconut mixture leaves the side of the pan easily (No syrup must running out), remove form the heat an beat with a spoon for 3-5 minutes.

4 Add the almond extract and food colouring of your choice, if desired.

5 Drop by spoon onto a greased tray for free form sugar cakes or put to cool in a glass dish and cut into squares.

6 Ready to eat

Author bio

Marva Carty is British-born, Caribbean bred and US/UK educated. She loves great stories, good jokes, Zumba and mangoes.

"Thank you for reading my book. I hope you enjoyed this story. As an independently published author, I appreciate your support. Please leave a rating on Amazon if you liked this book, or check out my first book,

"Mari Loves Mangoes"."

You can also join our mailing list at www.mangolimepublishing.com

to keep up to date with all our adventures.